Evincepub
Publishing

Evincepub Publishing

Nehru Nagar, Bilaspur, Chhattisgarh 495001
First Published by Evincepub Publishing 2021
Copyright © SUHAAN.J.KRISHNAN 2021
All Rights Reserved.
ISBN: 978-93-5446-221-4

The Book from heaven

THE LOST

WORLD OF HEAVENS

NOVEL WRITTEN BY

SUHAAN.J.KRISHNAN

Table of Contents

Chapter-1

Introduction

————•————

Dear reader friends, I am GERALD RENELEN. I live in New York with my sister named JANE RENELEN who is two years younger than me and my mother who is always busy, she is also busy during weekends but she gets leaves in public holiday like Christmas or Good Friday and all.

And I had a father whose name is Davidren; he had passed away recently due to some severe illness when I was only 7 years old. When he was going to the hospital I was really sad, so before leaving he turned to me and told me his last words- alone is what we feel inside but from the outside we are not at all alone.

Then he removed his locket which was around his neck, and tied it around my neck. After that he said- this locket will protect you from everything that is going to harm or disappoint you, so keep it with you son, and remember I am always with you. With that he went to the hospital with one last sad look at me.

And from that day onwards I have never removed this locket from my neck and now I have this lucky charm of his, which he gave me. Also there was some reason why he gave me this locket, which I don't remember.

This lucky charm is an oval shaped locket with something written in the middle which I cannot read because it has now became very old, almost like a fossil.

So in this story, if you have read the story name which is the lost world of heavens, then you have thought it right there is a place called heaven in this story. So it all started like this........

Chapter-2

Going to Pelham bay national park

It was one sunny day with very little clouds in the sky. When I was having my breakfast at 8:00AM in the morning, Jane suddenly came to me with a happy face and said- hey Gerald, how about going to Pelham bay national park? Because today is a fresh day to go for a walk there, so what do you think?

I thought for a moment and said- hmm, well maybe you are right, it is a fresh day, so, well, okay well then we will leave in ten minutes. She now got even happier and said okay quickly and left.

I ate my breakfast and was ready to go. After getting ready, we both sat on our bikes and took off. After about 20 minutes we finally reached Pelham bay national park.

We crossed the main gate and we reached inside the national park. I found out that there were so many people there. We started to walk there when Jane saw one of her friend there, so she turned to me and said- I am going with her okay, I will see you after a while. Then I said okay and she left.

 I also wished to see one of my friends or make one now, but no, everyone around was with someone else so I walked alone.

Jane was actually right! It was a great day at the national park. I walked slowly in between the shadows of the trees.

Suddenly I felt something strange! I felt something like vibration! And it was- It was coming from my neck! The locket!

Chapter-3

Magic words!

It really was my locket! The vibration somehow controlled my entire body! I was now walking, but it was not me, the locket made me walk somehow and somewhere!

I tried and tried but I couldn't stop myself from walking! While walking for a while I finally stopped where there was not even a single person standing, everything around was just trees! I was all alone here! Suddenly my locket glowed brightly in yellow colour!

I didn't care about the locket glowing instead I tried to walk back, but I couldn't! Suddenly my hands picked up my locket on its own, when I looked at it I saw that the word which was soiled was now clear! I could read it now!

I held it in my right hand and somehow I read it in a smooth and sweet voice: heaven world arise, I can hear you unhappy cries, I will arrive and save the day, so show and open the portal door I am on my way.

At that very moment the lockets light touched the air in front of me and drew a shape of a rectangle, and then a mythical door appeared! My hand was going to open the door on its own! When I touched the doorknob I felt a bit cold. I twisted the knob which made a creaking sound, and within seconds I opened the door. The door too opened with a creaking sound and I stepped inside the door.

And I found that everything around me was just white! Suddenly, under my leg, I felt some kind of a super huge pressure pushing me upward to the sky! But couldn't see the sky, as I told you everything around was white! I felt as if I was inside a white tunnel with some pressure which was making me move upward.

I was so scared that I thought I would die with fear! I was moving like topsy-turvy. I was screaming on top of my lungs! My locket was glowing brightly all this time! Then suddenly, I saw another door appear just a little far away from me. The door was colorful with the picture of a castle I have never seen before! Then when I was just close to it, it opened on its own! There were lights coming out of it, too bright for me to see so I covered my eyes with both my hands. I was still moving upward. When the door finally opened, I entered the door covering my eyes.

Chapter-4
When I opened my eyes…..

———·———

Now I felt like, I was slowly falling down. Then I landed very softly in the ground. The ground where I fell was so soft. When my heartbeat slowly slowed down, I felt like someone taping my forehead slowly, and when I opened my eyes, I saw a boy with very bright face almost like milk!

And blue eyes and a soft looking pointed nose, and he had bright white wings! I stood up and I was so scared looking at him. Now he squinted at my locket and turned to me in a surprised face and said proudly- are you davidren? Welcome back dear warrior!

I got confused and said to him in a surprised manner to him- warrior who? And from where I have returned? You look more like a bird or…..or……or…….an…..an…...angel!

His eyes widened then he asked me- don't you remember me oh warrior? Okay then I will explain, oops sorry I forgot to introduce myself; I am Angelias from the Angelean kingdom, our king and queen has called you to speak with you about something important, so we must go.

Where am I? I said in a scared manner. He smiled and said- sorry, I am a bit forgetful so I forgot to tell you something again, so let me clear my throat, ahem ahem, welcome to the lost world of heavens! But it may not be our world anymore. He said sadly.

I got curious and said in a little loud voice- heaven world! Did I die! I knew I would die in fear! I was just roaming in Pelham bay national park, how did I die?

He suddenly made a confusing face and said- No, you did not die oh warrior, you are called over here. Hearing that, I got so relaxed. We must get to the white diamond castle right away- he said. White diamond castle? I asked confusingly. I thought- does he mean the picture of a castle I saw in that door I entered? I wondered.

Yes, it's the name of the king and queen's castle he said. But I am a bit forgetful so I forgot some of the route, that's why we must use the mapper drop, he continued.

Mapper drop? I got confused I thought-now what is this new thing? Yes, it a drop of special water which is very difficult to create, this drop of water can make you see the way to any place you want to go, this drop is very hard to make, if you want to make it then you will have to add 289 different ingredients with water and leave the remaining solution alone undisturbed for one year and six months, then only you will get the mapper drop, but this drop works in an easy way, just put one drop of it in both of your eyes and close your eyes for three second and while that three seconds you will have to say or imagine the picture of the place in your mind then you will be able to see one path glowing in white color, just follow that glow until you see your destination.

I got shocked and said- ohh, I don't believe it but still let's go then.

He now gave me the mapper drop, and we both dropped one drop of the mapper drop in our eyes and closed our eyes for three second. In my mind I just said the words the white diamond castle. And then when I opened my eyes, it really worked out; I could see the way we had to go. There were three different ways in front of us; the way we had to go was glowing in white colour while the other ways were seen in dark colour. Angelias started to fly with his wings without carrying me! I shouted- Hey! Where are you going without me?

 Oops, sorry I forgot! I rolled my eyes. Then he carried me and we were going to the white diamond castle or whatever it is!

Chapter-5

The devil kingdom

It was a very beautiful sight; there were so many beautiful trees with different-different colors of leafs and flowers of the trees, almost infinite of them. Beautiful birds also of different colors flew all together somewhere. The colors of the tree leafs were pink, green, yellow, blue, violet, purple, red and much- much more! The sounds of the chirping birds made me feel relaxed and the fresh air made my heart happy! It felt like paradise!

Wow, this is so wonderful- I said to myself. Angelias smiled and said- isn't it beautiful, there are so many beautiful trees because these trees were killed or cut down without even finishing their full growth when they were on the earth!

I laughed and said- you're right actually, people are cutting down many trees for their own will, but there are some places were they protect them along with the wildlife like national park and wildlife sanctuary and all. Angelias smiled and continued the path.

While we were flying we saw a dark part of the land which had a creepy look. I looked there and asked Angelias- hey, why is that place looking a bit dark and creepy?

Angelias sighed and said- they are our enemies, they were the one who did everything wrong out here. I got confused so I was going to say what was wrong, but he looked sad for whatever the reason was, so I thought not to remind him about whatever the wrong thing is, so I kept silent. While flying Angelias's face expression changed as if he remembered something he forgot.

Hey I almost forgot to tell you dear warrior that, the king had told me to take you to the cursed peak and grab out your armor from there AND then only come to the white diamond castle! Angelias said.

I didn't understand what he said I wondered in my mind - armor? What is he talking about? And what does he mean by the cursed peak? It sounds scary! I didn't ask anything to him because if he replies anything, I can get even more confused! So I kept quiet again.

I don't know why but, after when he said that, he started flying even faster. While flying for a while he was about land, just aside of a dark and creepy looking mountain, soon he landed there on the side of the old creepy mountain.

Chapter-6

The story of the cursed peak

Angelias still had an unhappy face. Then he turned to me and said- this mountain is called the cursed peak, this mountain was first called the heavenly mountain, but as time passed it got changed.

How? I asked. It all started like this, he explained:

One beautiful day when davidren, meaning you were going to be given the award of being the most powerful warrior, you were going to be awarded the mighty warrior suit and the ultimate warrior sword, but just before you were being given, the devil kingdoms devils started to attack us, we all fought with all our might, but we were slowly losing, but you were the most powerful warrior so because of you the devil kingdoms army started losing, but that's when the real terror happened, the protector of the devil kingdom attacked us, the protector was an enormous mighty brown dragon with blood red eyes whose name is devilen, he was so powerful but you had fought with him for a while, but just then our protector dragon whose entire body is white and has blue eyes, had come to the rescue, but devilen was powerful so somehow he managed to tackle poor whiturn, devilen used his powers and made whiturn over his control, then you saw all of this and attacked devilen, but devilen grabbed you and throwed you to the earth, but with the help of our soldiers we pulled you up, but the devil soldiers attacked our soldiers and you fell right there but because of your locket you were safely landed on the earth, while you were falling, the king of the devils whose name is daredevil cursed whiturn and the curse was- whiturn should protect the mighty warrior suit and the ultimate warrior sword from getting into anyone's hands inside the heavenly peak, and if he didn't and if he tries to get away from there, then he will be killed and so the Angelean kingdom will turn weak, so he protected the suit and the sword for a long time, meanwhile the king of the Angelean kingdom turned devilen into a statue with the help of his three precious gems, and throwed devilen into to a hidden place on earth, the gems were attached to his spear, the gems are the sapphire, the ruby and the diamond, these three gems are really powerful with the diamond being the most powerful, they have the power of creating, destroying or cursing anything, but now our king is now a bit weak and now he has married to sparkle, whiturn is inside this mountain guarding the suit and the sword, king daredevil cursed whiturn to protect the suit and sword because if you wear it then you will have the power to kill devilen as the suit and the sword was made by the power of the three gems so you will have to enter this mountain, take the suit and the sword and prepare to face devilen. The three gems are in the earths most dangerous places, the ruby gem is in the most depth of the pacific ocean guarded by a ferocious sea creature called the megaledon and the sapphire is hidden in the mountain named Himalaya guarded by a monstrous creature called yeti and the diamond is in the core of the earth guarded by the hot lava, it is said that the lava is alive! But still the sapphire and the ruby got stolen by the soldiers and now if the diamond is also stolen, and if they three are put together in the space provided in the statue of devilen, then devilen will return because the space in the statue will use the power of all the three gems to bring devilen back to life, and if devilen returned he will destroy the entire heaven world and turn the heaven world into devil world! And they will also destroy the earth! This is the reason why this mountain is called the cursed peak instead of heavenly peak, you can break the curse with the help of your locket, so to protect this world we had to call you back because you are the only one who has the might to defeat devilen so you will have to protect us oh davidren warrior.

I was so shocked when I heard this that's why I kept my hand in my heart and said- I will save the heaven world for sure but one thing I want to tell you that I am not davidren my father was davidren, my name is Gerald renelen my father has passed away because he had some kind of disease, but whatever it is I will defiantly save the world of heavens. Angelias smiled and said thank you so much warrior, come on now let's go inside.

Chapter-7

Entering the cursed peak

So, how do we enter in this mountain? I asked Angelias.

It's easy, you just touch the wall with one of your hand, and then it will open on its own he said. I said okay and I was going to touch the walls of this mountain.

I raised my hand and I touched the wall with my entire hand. But nothing happened, but after a while the surprising thing happened!

The wall started to change its colour into yellow colour which was moving like an ocean wave, and then it started to vibrate, after three seconds of vibration, the wall changed into its normal colour and it moved to the left side, so I removed my hand and let the wall move. The wall stopped after a while.

It was dark there inside. Oh no, now why it's so dark in here? And what if whiturn attack us? I asked Angelias.

But suddenly my locket started to glow in yellow, that's why now I could see everything inside clearly, but I could not see some part of the way.

I entered the mountain. It was very long and narrow inside. Then suddenly I felt like some light reflecting somewhere, I looked closer, and saw the armor suit and the sword! We both looked at each other for two seconds smiling, and when I was going to step forward Angelias grabbed my shoulder and reminded me that whiturn will come to attack you in any time, so move slowly towards the suit and the sword.

The suit and the sword looked so amazing that it looked like only a god could wear it! So when I was moving forward I heard sound of rocks falling on the ground! I turned left and saw two dark blue eyes!

But I could not see its body; its eyes were locked on mine. Angelias suddenly looked a bit frightened and said- beware oh warrior davidren, I mean Gerald, he is not like the old whiturn now, so be careful.

Suddenly it started to come out from the dark spot and I saw a large white beautiful and scary looking dragon, after looking at me for a while, he started to look in my locket for three seconds and stared at me. Then he came closer to me and raised his hand towards my locket. His hand came closer and closer when I stopped him by saying- hey, what are you doing?

Whiturn heard what I said and made an unhappy face and said to me- please oh warrior, may I get out of this curse please, I can understand you, oh warrior Gerald, I heard you speak to angelias about everything.

I got surprised and said- okay then; I will let you out of this curse, so how do I do it? It's easy; you and I just have to hold your locket together.

Okay then let's do it I said. Now I held my hands in my locket whiturn also held it, then we both closed our eyes. I was imagining that my locket would glow again and it would get whiturn out of this curse, after a while, when I opened my eyes, what I imagined started to happen!

My locket glowed brightly and its lights were moving to whiturns body and he got transformed into a whiter body and his dark blue eyes became even brighter. Then slowly-slowly the locket turned into its real normal form.

Whiturn looked even more strong and powerful, and especially he looked even mightier!

Chapter-8

Continuing our way

Whiturn gave me a hand shake and said-thank you very much all mighty warrior. I smiled and said-you're very welcome, now let's go to the white diamond castle before it is too late.

Whiturn suddenly became sad and he said- I am sorry dear warrior, but I can't, if I come along with you, then the devil soldiers might find me and they will capture and curse me again, so I will have to stay here.

I felt sad and said its okay to him. Then I went to wear the suit and grab the sword. I walked confidently toward it.

Every time when I take a step forward, nearer to the armor and sword, I feel a strike of confidence in my heart. Finally, when the armor and the sword was just a step forward, I reached my hand to touch it, I felt a strong feeling of both diamond and unbreakable metal when I touched it.

Just when I wore it, my locket glowed brightly for a second, and at the same time I felt like my muscles increasing and was growing stronger and stronger, which made me feel that I was really a true warrior, I could feel it and now I got the spirit of making the heaven world happy again.

I don't know why but it felt even easier to walk, for me now, it was comfortable to wear it, when though it was made of both metal and diamond. But from the outside it didn't look like it was made of metal or diamond at all! I didn't know why.

We both said- good bye to whiturn and we moved out of the mountain. Again Angelias carried me and we continued our way to the white diamond castle.

While we were flying, I thought to take a look at the mountain once again, so I looked behind and saw that the mountain which had been looking creepy had now become a bit white, only a bit, I think it is getting its real form again. It looks like now it is going to turn into the heavenly mountain again- I thought.

So as we flied for a long time, we saw a huge and enormous white gate below us. We also saw that the other side of the gate was extremely cloudy, so we could only see some part of the land of angels through the small holes present between thc clouds.

After a while Angelias landed in front of the gate gently. We went closer and closer to the gate, that's when an angel came walking near to us and gave us a strange look. Angelias whispered to me that he is trying to figure out whether we are a devil or an angel. After 7 seconds of examining he smiled and welcomed us.

He let us pass through the gate. When the gate opened, it didn't even make a single creaking sound as it opened! I don't know why but I got happy when the gate opened and also when i entered the kingdom.

When we were walking in the kingdoms marketing place, angelias said that- this suit now you are wearing has now made you 50% Gerald and 50% davidren, which means your fathers 50% spirit is in that suit, so sometimes it can control you or your feelings or your entire body or anything, but the only difference is that you can control yourself only of 50%, and your locket even had a name which I recently forgot! But don't worry; maybe someone in the castle will know what its name was. I rolled my eyes again. How forgetful he is! I thought.

He also told me that my locket can protect me and also give me good luck as long as it is in my neck, he also he told me why this heaven world is called the lost world, it is so called because at first, this world was on the earth billions of years ago, but soon we found out that human are going to developing technology which can pollute and destroy both the heaven world and thee earth, so to protect itself, the angels used there magical powers which transferred the heaven world into the sky after making itself not visible for humans, but still humans can come here after their death.

As we moved on, we saw a very beautiful sight, it was huge, it was white, and it was an amazing looking castle!

Chapter-9

The white diamond castle

This is the white diamond castle Angelias said pointing his hand to the castle. I was still somehow happy by seeing the white diamond castle.

We were going closer to the entrance of the castle, that's when two guards in front of the huge door stopped us! When they just stopped us my locket again glowed brightly for two seconds, in that two seconds time, the light of the locket touched both the two guard's heads and their eyes also glowed at that time and after that two seconds of glowing, their eyes were as they were before again after two seconds.

They blinked for a while and said in a proud way- a very warm welcome to the white diamond castle!

Angelias then looked at me with a cool look and said- told you that it will give you good luck.

We entered the door and what we saw all around was just diamond, that too with white colour! Now I understood how this castle got its name, because everything around looks likes white diamond only!

We passed through the way which leads to the king and queens court, it was really beautiful inside. As we walked we found a huge beautiful door, we passed through the door and found out that the king and queen was reading a book, but as they heard the door opening sound, they looked forward and stood up after closing the book.

They smiled at us, as if they were waiting for us all the time! King spark said in a surprised and happy manner- welcome back dear warrior, we were so worried about you, welcome back. The queen also welcomed us after the king.

Before they could say anything else I hesitated- Okay let me just say, before you say something else, let me tell you that I am not davidren; I am Gerald, davidren's son, so please call me Gerald the most powerful warrior, not davidren the powerful warrior!

The King smiled at me and said- off course you are, it just that you might have forgotten everything because you have been in earth for so long, we will first treat you because you might be tired on the way of your return and then we will train you in facing devilen.

I gulped and nodded to the king. Okay fine!

Chapter-10

Training

The king and queen led us to a room with a huge and long table, we were then treated with amazing foods, and then we took rest for a while. After a while one of the guards called me and took me to the training Centre with Angelias.

First the trainer teached me horse riding which I did successfully and next was sword fighting which every time when my trainer tries to defeat me, my locket glows and he gets defeated!

In every training event this happens and my trainer gets defeated! So it was really easy in defeating him, then suddenly my trainer was extremely tired and said to me- it's better not to train you because it seems impossible in defeat you, as you have your locket, so I suggest when you are going to fight with devilen, you just have to believe in yourself because your locket will protect you from every danger you are going to face as long as it will be in your neck.

I smiled and when closer to my trainer and held his hand in my locket and closed my eyes. While my eyes were closed I imagined that my locket will glow brightly and recover the tiredness of the trainer, and then as soon as I opened my eyes what I imagined had happened!

The locket glowed brightly in yellow colour and the lights moved to the trainer body and soon after a while the colour disappeared from the trainer's body and he looked more energetic!

Then he smiled at me and thanked me many times. After a while, he stopped thanking and told me to sit with him, when we sat on a nearby bench, he started telling me everything about my locket!

Chapter-11

The story of the immordilean

My trainer made an unhappy face and started telling me the story of my locket it all started one day, long-long ago, the heaven world was on the earth, it was a beautiful place there, not a single problem or difficulties were created , there were beautiful trees, places, sights beautiful everything,

but that's when the disaster happened, the kings three powerful gems which is the ruby, the sapphire and the diamond was acting really strange, the king found out that the entire heaven world was going to get destroyed that's why the gems acted really weird, the cause of the destruction was that, evil people was going to be born and they will destroy everything by polluting the air, water and land, so to protect our self's we used the power of all the three gems to create a new magical thing which can protect the heaven world, so we created an incredibly powerful locket which has the power of good luck, so we created it and we used the power of it to move the heaven world into the sky and make it disappear, we called it the almighty locket the immordilean. Only a kind person can enter the heaven world, but there were still some animals and trees which were not able to come here, so again with the help of the immordilean we used its power and made such that if they die on the earth, then it can come here and live. So in the kingdom of Angelean, we decided to conduct a competition which will decide the most powerful warrior, which came to known as the royal warrior and the royal warrior is the one who owns the immordilean which is now you, that's why I am warning you, protect your immordilean from king daredevils hands because it is almost more powerful than the three gems so you should really protect it or this world will be nothing but dust.

Hearing the story I got really surprised and shocked thinking about my locket, I mean the immordilean. My trainer held my hand and gave me a handshake, then he said- good luck, you will have to face devilen, but don't worry I will tell you a secret.

He looked everywhere around in a strange face expression as if trying to make sure that no one is around, after a while he continued- the only thing you will have to do is bclieve in yourself and the rest your immordilean will do it, because it is said that the immordilean is alive and will protect the one who is wearing it, but because it is made by the three gems, it will always support positive in another words, it protects the heaven world, but this does not mean that if evil people wear it then it will not obey the evil person, because there are some magical spells which can stop the immordilean from protecting the heaven world and there are so many spells which can convert it into evil or good and most importantly there are magical things which can even remove the immordilean from your neck, which you may think is impossible! You may also think that before anyone tries to remove it, it will glow and stop that person from removing it, but this is not true, there are things which can remove it without any incident!

So I repeat while you are fighting with devilen, you just have to believe in yourself and also sometimes your immordilean can control your body which mean that davidren will fight devilen not you, that's why the immordilean is called alive as your fathers spirit is inside it. You might have wondered- if my father has died in the earth, then why didn't he return in the heaven world, right? Well, you are right, he was supposed to be born here once again but he never wanted to leave you alone so he entered in your immordilean! As he finished the story of the immordilean I got very-very shocked and surprised to hear that my father is very close to me!

As we were talking my trainer suddenly saw Angelias behind me, just then he made an small angry face said in a little loud voice-aaii! What are you doing here listening to our secret!

Angelias smiled and said-okay-okay I will not tell it to anyone. Now my trainer made an expression of a detective and said- hmm fine I will believe you.

Suddenly one of the guards of the white diamond called me and Angelias. The guard came closer to us and said- oh royal warrior, the king and queen has called you. I and Angelias looked at each other for a moment and we started walking after saying good bye to the trainer.

The guard led us to the place where there were the king and queen. The Guard called them and the king and the queen looked at us, the queen said to angelias in a sweet voice- did you observe the royal warriors training?

Angelias nodded smiling and said- yes of course I did. So how was the training? The queen asked. It was amazing; the trainer didn't even win the training challenge even for once!

Now the king and queen laughed in a small voice's. Slowly they stopped laughing and the king said something to both of us.

Chapter-12

Journey through the earth's core

So, warrior, you now have mission to complete, you will have to go to the earth's core and bring the diamond gem here.

I got curious and asked but how do we get there? And even if I get there I will return being a fried human!

The queen laughed a little and said- don't worry warrior, we have the solution for that. She came right in front of me and raised her hand in my locket I mean the immordilean and touched it. The immordilean glowed for one second and became normal.

The queen smiled at me and said- there now no matter how hot or how cold is the place you go, you won't get hurt, you will be at normal temperature!

I smiled and asked both king and queen so how do we get there?

The king suddenly looked at me and said- follow me I will show you.

I and Angelias followed the king, the queen didn't come with us, but before leaving king and queen's court, she said good bye to us. So only me, Angelias, king spark and 6 soldiers surrounding the king were walking there. King spark led us outside the entrance of the castle.

I wondered where we were going. While walking for 2 minutes, we finally reached behind the castle where we stopped. There was a wooden door which had a hole-like thing in the center. The hole was surrounded by some small black line pipes which connected the hole. The pipes were in the size of a pencil.

The king looked at me and said- go ahead dear warrior. I thought for a while and asked the king- um, okay, but what should I do?

The king made a confusing face and said- I think you forgot what to do, okay let me tell you; this door is called the heavenly transporter, this door will take you to the center of the earth, only the person who is wearing the immordilean can us it, like you, now all you have to do is blast your immordileans power beam in that hole and say where you wish to go in your mind, then it will open and you will reach that place in a jiffy!

(A power beam is a beam of magic, power and strength. If a blasted power beam touches something, then it may break or get damaged. A power beam can come out of a dragon's mouth, a magical spear, the three powerful gems, the immordilean and much more powerful things!)

I said okay and pointed my immordilean in that hole, I said the words the earth's core in my mind after closing my eyes and also imagined that a power beam is coming out of the immordilean. As soon as I imagined that, I felt small vibration in the immordilean!

And when I opened my eyes, I saw that a yellow power beam was coming out the immordilean and touched the hole in the door. I saw that the small black pipes slightly glowed in yellow. After a while the door opened, we couldn't see anything inside the door as it was glowing brightly in yellow. I stopped the immordileans power beam and passed through the door with Angelias after saying good bye to the king!

Chapter-13

Where is Angelias?

I entered inside the door and really I didn't feel any hotness, I felt like the same temperature inside the white diamond. I think my locket helped me to adjust the heat in here. The door closed behind me and disappeared.

Everything around was just lava and lava and some rocks. I smiled and turned around to Angelias, but he was not there! I looked everywhere and also at the same time I shouted Angelias multiple times but it was no use.

That's when I suddenly heard sounds of someone grunting! It was coming from the ground! So when I looked down, I saw Angelias!

He was all red and his tongue was outside his mouth, his wings were red too and he looked like he was going to die because of heat!

I got shocked and said- oops, sorry I forgot about you. I then used my immordileans power and made him also heat proof. After I made him heat resistant with my immordilean, he was breathing through his mouth loudly, and gasping loudly for a while!

Oh my god, the heat nearly killed me, thank you davidren, oops I mean Gerald! I rolled my eyes and said ok then let's go find the diamond gem. Angelias nodded and said yeah let's go.

Chapter-14

Where is the diamond gem?

We were walking and walking for a long time and in between every time when Angelias gets tired, he says- we will have to complete the mission before the devil knight finds it.

While I was walking my immordilean started to shine! It was shining like a bulb turning on and off and on and off again and again! Angelias and I made a confused face and stared at the immordileans light.

It now started to act really-really strangely. That's when Angelias's eyes widened; suddenly he said to me in a very low voice- oh-no no-no, your immordilean is trying to warn us that we are being spied by someone or something!

I turned around and saw a small rock which was going to fall down a cliff which was at the top, it was moving fast because of the slop, then at last it fell down, then it landed at the tip of the dead end of the rock we were standing! It stopped right at the tip of the dead end which leads to the boiling lava!

By seeing that I gasped and said to Angelias in a small voice- hey why are we just walking in circles just like that? Why can't we just use the mapper drop!

Angelias's eyes widened even larger and laughingly he slapped his forehead and said- hahaha you are right, you're really-really right I didn't even think about that, looks like you have really good memory. I smiled and muttered actually it's not true but still let's consider that as the truth for now! Come on let's go.

Chapter-15

Tracking the diamond gem

Angelias took out the mapper drop and dropped one drop of it in both of his eyes and then he closed his eyes and gave me the small bottle of it, I also dropped a drop of it in my eyes and closed it for a while and then I opened my eyes and saw the path glowing slightly in white color, and so, we both together followed the path.

Every time in between I feel strange, like I keep getting a funny feeling about something!

Now we were walking for a long time when suddenly, we stopped in front of a dead end which is in front of a large rock which had many-many dusty pictures and drawings of something!

In the middle of the rock was an oval shape just like my locket! And everywhere around it were the pictures of ferocious lava showing that the diamond gem was deep inside the lava!

Angelias's mouth widened slightly and he observed the pictures by squinting hard at it and then suddenly he said- this is it-this is it, I think you need to press your locket inside that little hole, and I think after that only will the diamond gem will come out of the lava.

After when he said that, I also observed the pictures for a while and then said to Angelias- hmm, it looks like your right, well then; let's try doing that for once.

Angelias and I looked at each other for two seconds and then I removed my immordilean from my neck and pressed it into the hole after blowing away some dust inside the hole.

After when I pressed it inside, nothing happened for two seconds, but after two seconds, my immordilean glowed brightly in yellow and then suddenly the entire picture in the wall also glowed in the same colour of the lava, except the picture of the diamond, it glowed in white colour!

The picture of the diamond glowed really bright, and then its light flied out of the picture and touched the middle of the lava, which I think that made the lava jump vigorously, and then suddenly it happened!

The thing we were looking for was coming out! From where the light touched, from that place itself something was rising! Slowly-slowly it came out of the lava. What I mean by the word `it' of that sentence means the diamond gem!

The diamond gems pictures lights were still touching the real diamond gem. It finally stopped after a while.

The diamond gem was so-so beautiful that I felt like I should always and always stay or live forever with it! It was not like other diamonds, it was so clean, so shiny and so sharp looking gem. That gem is perfect to be called as the `god-made gem'! we both kept looking at it for a while with relaxed expressions!

After a while a bridge made of stone was formed. The bridge was formed perfectly and nicely.

Angelias and I looked at each other smiling, and we were about to go grab the diamond gem when suddenly a little loud voice spoke-

Wow, you both at last found the gem which we were looking for! I am the one who is going to take the gem, oh, and yes, you may call me the knight of king daredevil!

Chapter-16

Oh-no, not you!

I got extremely startled by hearing that voice and turned around, and saw what we didn't expect, the devil soldiers and a knight!

The knight chuckled and in a scary voice he said- thank you thank you so much for leading us to diamond gem, now step aside and let me grab it!

I ran to grab my immordilean and grabbed it as fast as I can, and then I quickly tossed it around my neck.

No wonders I was feeling weird and the immordilean glowed like that!

The devil knight started to walk nearer to the diamond gem, to take it! I told Angelias- look, I'II take care of the knight you just distract the devil soldiers, okay.

Angelias said okay and then he started to fly to the devil soldiers.

I ran to the bridge and stepped in front of the knight. He stopped and looked at my locket with wide eyes for three seconds and then he said to me- ohh, looks like the poor old davidren has_

But before he could answer I interrupted I am his son, Gerald renelen! The knight looked surprised and said- ahh, I see-I see, now step aside and let me take it or else you will lose your little friend!

I got a little afraid and also little shocked. The knight moved to the left side and he showed me something which I didn't expect!

It was Angelias! He was shouting help again and again because he was captured by the devil soldiers!

The knight looked at me and said- so, dear son of davidren, what do you suggest? Do you wish that I make your little angel friend into a devil with my powers, or do you wish to give me the diamond gem, huh?

I got really confused and terrified, what should I do? I was thinking and thinking hard for a while, then soon after a while I said in a sad and angry voice- fine, leave him alone and I will let you take it!

Just when I said that, the knight made an evil smile and made the soldiers let him go. They let him go and then I moved aside.

The knight raised his hand towards the shining gem, but there was something else in his hand, he had two metal rods in both of his hands, he used the tip of the metal rods to take the diamond gem and soon he did.

But why did he use two metal rods instead of his hands? (You will soon find it out why he did that!) He then turned around and with some kind of magic he had, he made a tunnel on the rock which was high top of us, he then flew away in that tunnel with his soldiers.

Angelias came running to me and then he started to apologize to me many-many times, and as for me what could I say?

I just said yeah, it's okay again and again. I asked Angelias sadly- now what?

Angelias then looked around and then he spotted the hole in which the knights and the soldiers went away, then he turned to me, and by pointing his fingers to the hole he said-hey don't lose hope, we still have a chance, let's now go and stop the knights and the soldiers from bringing devilen back!

After hearing that I sighed and got a little happy and was going to do what he said.

Chapter-17

Following the devil warriors

Angelias grabbed my hand and started to fly, I also flew with him as he grabbed me.

It was a long-long hole. After flying for a very-very long time I finally saw light coming out from somewhere on top.

I think it took a long time because we were at the earth's core. The light came out of another hole which I think was the exit from this tunnel and the earth's core.

We then finally came out of the hole. We realized that we in the middle of a huge forest. There was no sign of the devil warrior's, so I got disappointed.

I sighed and said to Angelias- well, now what?

Angelias looked all around and said in a frightened voice now we will defiantly have to find those knights before they make devilen come back to life!

I stared at angelias for three seconds and said- well, we are in the middle of a huge forest right now so how will we find them now?

Angelias was just going to answer something, but suddenly my immordilean glowed and its light touched the ground, and also at the same time something weird had happened to me!

Something made me tell Angelias that we should follow the light of the immordilean! So I told him that, and we were about to follow the light when suddenly Angelias asked me why should we follow the light.

With a confused voice I replied- I think the immordilean made me say that, now let's stop wasting time, come on, we will fly and follow it so that the devil soldiers and the knight don't spot us.

Angelias said okay and then he flew away, he also carried me.

The light was sometimes moving to the left or right on its own, and the surprising thing here is that I didn't even turn it to the left or right with my hands!

So, while flying and flying we finally spotted the devil warriors!

We both landed and followed them by hiding. They were walking a bit fast so we also had to move fast. They all finally stopped right in front a huge mountain.

The knight then walking forward and took out the diamond gem, and made it touch the mountain slightly.

Suddenly the diamond gem glowed and its light touched the mountain, and at the same time, something strange happened, the entire mountain began to vibrate!

Then the mountain began to crack, it kept cracking for a while. Suddenly the mountain stopped vibrating and then we found out that the cracks made on the mountain looked like a huge rectangle; it looked just like a door! And I was right!

The door was soon formed, but the difference was that it was an open door it didn't had any closings on it. I found out that there was some kind of writings of top of the open door;

It read The dungeon of devils! That made me a bit frightened.

The knight made an evil laugh and went inside the huge door. I sighed again and then turned to Angelias and found out that, he was now looking scared out of his wits! I didn't want him to be scaried, so I grabbed his hand and pulled him inside the door.

Angelias replied stammering sh-sh-should w-we ha-have t-to do I-it?!

Then I said yes in a loud voice. Angelias once again replied in a stammering voice d-do yo-you even kn-know tha-that dev-dev-devilen is about to_

But before he could say something else i tightened his hand and walked pass the huge door with Angelias behind me. I must say, his hands were shivering and was very cold!

Chapter-18

Inside dungeon of devils

I passed the door with Angelias behind me; he was still shivering and had a frightened face.

As we walked, we saw the knight and the soldiers. They were also walking forward like us. So, as we walked we saw a huge cage, which was extremely dark inside, the only bright thing inside was two parallel round blood-red lights coming from the inside. It looked very scary, as if it was someone's eyes!

The cage was almost bigger than the entrance door of this mountain. The knight and the soldiers stopped by seeing the cage.

By seeing the cage, the knight took the diamond gem and pointed the diamond gem to the cage.

By doing that, the diamond gem started to glow and then its light touched the cage which made the entire cage made of steel break into pieces!

They all entered the dark part of the corner and somehow they made the diamond gem glow, which showed the way, it was a tunnel.

I once again grabbed Angelias's arm and got inside the tunnel. Angelias was staring deeply at the red lights, at the same time, it looked like the lights was staring back at him!

When I took the first step in the tunnel, I had this strange feeling about something, even the immordilean was acting weird. It made me feel even stranger.

So, as we walked we heard the sound of the knight making evil laughter. Angelias quickly grabbed me by the shoulder.

He was now looking really scared because this time the knight's laughter was even eviler than the first time he laughed before entering the door of this mountain or the dungeon of devils.

That made me feel even weird as if like something terrible was going to happen! Something terribly wrong!

Chapter-19

The evil looking statue

As I walked I saw something shining.

There were three lights which were coming out. The lights were red, white, and white with outlines of blue. Which I think was the ruby, the diamond and the sapphire gem!

We both peeked in the cave where the lights were coming from. As we peeked, we saw something really strange and scary!

The gems were flying in mid-air and there was a huge black statue of a huge powerful dragon-like thing! The dragon was slightly bigger than whiturn himself!

I got curious about that statue so I asked Angelias whether he knew anything about it. I asked him- what's that?

He then replied, tha-that's devilen o-only! I turned to the statue for once with really wide eyes, and maybe it was my imagination but still I saw that the statue was staring at me angrily with red glowing eyes, which I saw from the outside of the cage!

I saw that the knight was making the gems stick right below the statue; there were some space also for the gems to enter.

The gems now were flying just in front of that gem sticking space. The gems were getting closer and closer to the space every second! Then finally after a while the gems got stuck in the space and they were glowing vigorously!

Then suddenly something strange and scary happened. The entire dungeon of Devil Mountain began to vibrate! Some rocks even landed down from the top.

But that was no stranger than what happened to the statue! The statue began to break! It looked like some pieces of black dust were getting removed from the skin of a real dragon! It actually looked like that!

The Arm of the dragon statue looked like its dust completely got removed! Because of that the entire statue was going turn into………. a real powerful dragon!

Chapter-20

The return of ………..!

All the dust which made the dragon look like a statue broke free which means the entire dust got removed!

The thing now left after the dust got removed was a real dragon who was none other than………..devilen! He roared really loud that it made the entire mountain shake for 5 seconds! His glowing eyes turned back to normal.

Then he looked down to the knight and said loudly- yes, i am free now, how I hated to live inside that statue! Now I am free! It's time to rule over the heaven world, thank you devil knight!

I squinted at devilen and muttered- not on my watch will you rule over heaven world!

I then turned to Angelias and…….. Yes, your right he looked really afraid now.

So I used the power of the immordilean to calm him down. Then he did calm down.

Meanwhile in the white diamond castle, the king found out about this and whispered- oh-no!

Devilen then grabbed the three gems which made more powerful than anything! Then he started to fly with his wings. The knight jumped on his back and flew away!

I bend down to my knees and sighed a lot and thought- oh-no, what have I done? I promised to the king and queen that I will save the heaven world and now what?

After I thought that, my immordilean glowed brighly and its light went to the left side of me.

It didn't stop till now. i was too upset to turn around and see what my immordilean was doing. Then suddenly Angelias tapped his hands in my shoulder and said what happened? Angelias continued- come on

Gerald, there is someone who wishes to meet you!

My eyes went wide, and then I turned and saw something miraculous!

Chapter-21

The message from my father (davidren)!

Yes, the chapter name reads right it was my father being projected by the immordilean!

My father smiled and said to me- don't be afraid son, and don't think you are alone, I am always and forever with you, the immordilean will protect you whenever you are in trouble, and once again, don't think you are alone because me and your angel friend who is angelias and the immordilean is always with you, okay?

Now go defeat that dragon, in between I will control your body and will help you fight with devilen okay?

My eyes were wide and my mouth was also open. I replied to my father stammering- o-okay dad, now I-I am confident; I w-will keep my promise which I gave to the k-king and queen by defeating that devilen in p-place of you!

I said that stammering because I didn't believe that my dad who had passed away was now in front of me!

My father smiled and said `that's my brave boy' the protected figure from the immordilean disappeared. I wiped a tear out of eyes.

I took a large breath with my mouth and said to Angelias- okay we need to stop them right now!

Then Angelias said proudly- yeah, I know, come on, I will carry you, let's fly with my wings and catch them. I nodded and we both began to fly with me carried by Angelias.

Chapter-22

Meanwhile in the white diamond castle

Oh-no, I feel it- I feel it, devilen has returned! The King said to queen sparkle. He continued he has returned!

Queen sparkle said- no, this is bad; this is very-very bad.

The king said No-no it's okay, I know that davidren and…… I mean Gerald and Angelias will defeat them, I know that!

Let's see what they are doing out there, they obviously might be in the dungeon of devils because that's where devilen is, right? So let's use my magic to see them.

The queen said- but what if they see us? If devilen see's us, he might harm not only us but also the entire heaven world!

Don't worry, in this type of magic, they will not be able to see us but we can see them, also by watching them what they are doing, we can make sure that devilen is defeated.

The queen said okay, that's a good idea, now let's do it. He nodded and grabbed his spear and said some magic words.

That made the tip of the spear glow. The light touched the wall just aside of the king and queen. It projected and showed whatever we were doing in the next chapter, which is chapter-23 to chapter-32! They saw everything like a movie!

Chapter-23

Our mission!

—◆—

Angelias and I were flying, following devilen. While we were flying, I asked Angelias where they are going.

(We didn't know that we were being spied by the king and queen!)

Don't you know that? They are going to our kingdom to rule there! Angelias said in a little loud voice. Okay then let's somehow make them fall down- I said.

Angelias replied yeah that's a good idea! I was thinking and thinking how to make them fall, and suddenly the immordilean glowed as if to warn me of something. Its light made my hand move automatically!

I mean that, I didn't move them; it was as if the immordilean made me do that!

My hand grabbed the immordilean and it pointed to the devil people. This made the immordileans power beam blast to devilen, and trusts me, that made the entire dragon fall in the ground!

The beam disappeared when it made them fall.

They all landed in the ground with a thud. So, we also landed in the ground safely. We were a bit far away from them.

I saw that even though devilen fell down he looked like didn't get hurt at all! Slowly they all stood up, and with a surprising face, devilen and the knight saw us!

Chapter-24

You can never stop us!

Devilen spoke in a scary voice as usual- ah, I see that somebody is here to save the heaven world, but I am not letting that happen, and you can never stop us! Look, I have the three gems now, so I have the right to use the power of it, I will rule over the entire heaven world.

After saying that, he laughed. Then suddenly something mysterious happened, the immordilean glowed and its gas-like thing which came out of the immordilean entered my forehead! I tried to stop them but it was no use!

After a while the gas-like thing disappeared and my eyes glowed in yellow colour, like the immordileans glowing color as usual.

Now my entire body was not of my control! It was as if I was being controlled by my father!

I moved towards devilen, even though I didn't want to! Devilens eyes grew wide for 3 seconds and then he squinted at me, then his eyes went back to normal. He spoke- ahh, hello davidren! It's nice to see you after years!

I couldn't believe it! Devilen was seeing me as my father! I spoke in my father's voice- it's nice to see you too, and as usual I will not let you rule over the heaven world!

Chapter-25

Fight!

The diamond gem in Devilens neck glowed and its power beam was going to attack me!

So, as I was saying, the diamond gems power beam came near to us very fast, but before I could hurt myself, my father who was controlling my body swung the shield which was in my right hand.

(The armor which I took from the cursed peak was with me this whole time). The shield protected me from the harmful power beam.

He tried to eat me, he moved his entire mouth towards me but I moved aside, I mean my father moved aside!

He gave out a strong red power beam blast from his mouth, but I escaped again.

Every time his eyes glows in red color before the power beam was going to blast out of his mouth.

Devilen quickly backed me to a huge rock which was far behind me.

I was now leaning in the rock because he had pushed me so hard. I must say devilen was really quick and it seems like only a great warrior can defeat him.

Devilen came closer and closer to my face until my nose almost touched his mouth. Then he started talking to me- ha-ha, I love it when you look angry davidren, I love it very much!

I think devilen saw my father getting angry, that's why he said that.

Devilen continued- but don't worry my dear davidren; your anger won't last forever, because I am now going to turn that anger into sadness as the heaven world will be ruled by me!

After saying all this he laughed for a while and stopped. Devilen opened his mouth and I knew what was going to happen, he was going to blast out a power beam from his mouth.

But before he could do that the immordilean glowed brighly. Right at that moment something incredible happened! I felt a huge amount of air in my left side! When I turned left I saw the amazing moment happen!

Chapter-26

Whiturn to the rescue!

It was whiturn! He flew with his wings with all his might and blasted out a strong blast of power beam which hit devilen!

That made devilen blast away from me. He got crashed in another rock.

And meanwhile this entire thing was happening, angelias was fighting with the knight, but he didn't use any sword as he didn't have any swords, he was fighting with his wings, he snatched the sword from the knight and attack him by throwing rocks at him, and the surprising thing here is that, he was able to lift a huge rock which was almost bigger than him!

This might be happening because he should be angry that last time he had been captured by them and so he might wanted to take revenge!

Devilen slowly stood up. Then he started finding who blasted him for two seconds and then he found out. He saw whiturn.

Devilen made an evil smile. He was smiling at whiturn. Devilen started speaking. I was very-very surprised for what he said right now!

Chapter-27

Hello brother!

He said in a scary voice- hello brother! Yes, you read that right! It seemed like whiturn and devilen were nothing but……….brothers!

Devilen continued- it's nice to see you again, looks like davidren freed you from the curse I had given you!

I was now a bit angry because from the moment I came to this world I was telling everyone so many times that I am not davidren, I am Gerald, Gerald renelen, but it seemed like they were seeing me as davidren. When whiturn came here, Angelias looked very amazed! Angelias came flying to me, and then he turned to whiturn. Whiturn nodded to Angelias without saying a word and after that Angelias also nodded, and then he turned to me. Then whiturn started to fight devilen with all his might.

Meanwhile Angelias and I were discussing about how to defeat devilen! This means that we were making a plan!

Chapter-28

Our plan!

———•———

Whiturn was fighting with devilen while Angelias and I were hiding in a place making a plan.

Angelias explained to me- okay, the first thing we must do is remove the three gems from Devilens neck, then we must destroy one of the gems, because devilen was cursed by the power of all the three gems, this means that if we destroy one of the gems then devilen will never return as all the three gems are needed to bring him back, so I repeat we must destroy one of the gems, as there are no other way to defeat devilen other than that.

I looked at devilen for three seconds and replied to angelias- yeah, but how do we destroy the gem?

Angelias replied-it is said that only the power beam of your immordilean can destroy the gems, so you can use it, all you have to do is make the immordilean point to one of the gems and then imagine that its power beam is moving towards one of the gems, that's all you have to do.

We both smiled with happiness to Angelias and we both gave each other a high five and at the same time we both together said in a loud voice- let's do it!

Chapter-29

The first step

We both jumped out from our hiding place and we tried to do the first step.

Angelias suddenly spoke very quickly- I will be right back okay, at that time you can use the power beams right away, quick!

I was going to ask Angelias where he was going but it was too late, he had already flown away.

So, I looked at the immordilean for a while and did what angelias said, I slowly placed the immordilean in my right hand and pointed it to devilen who was still fighting with whiturn, I closed my eyes and imagined that some harmful power beams were coming out of the immordilean, and when I opened my eyes, it started to glow and some yellow lights came out of the immordilean and moving towards devilen,

But when the lights were moving towards devilen, a huge rock fell from the sky and it was going to pass through the power beam but no.

When the rock touched the power beam of the immordilean, the rock also started to move towards devilen.

This means that the power beam pushed the rock which was just in front of the power beam!

Devilen shouted nooo, as the rock crashed over him, which made the rock break into pieces!

My mouth was wide open! It took me a while to realize that, the rock was thrown by Angelias who was now flying in the sky!

Maybe this is why he had quickly flown away. When the rock crashed over devilen the three gems flew away from Devilens neck!

That's why Devilen once again shouted `no'. Devilen quickly stood up and tried to take the gems but whiturn somehow made devilen move away from the gems!

I was really proud of whiturn and Angelias. Angelias soon landed on the ground and said-this was the reason why I had flown away!

I told Angelias that I was very proud of both whiturn and him, and we were about to do the second step!

Chapter-30

The second step

———◆———

I ran to the gems which were now lying in the ground. But Angelias stopped me real quick.

No-no, don't touch the gems with your hands you may hurt yourself.

I got curious and asked- I have two question to you, what do you mean and how will I get hurt by myself?

Angelias replied- yeah I will tell you, no-one can touch or take the three of the gems because if you touch it, your hands will burn to ashes, only a true person who wishes to guard and protect the heaven world and is very honest can touch it without getting hurt, which is your father who is not here now, the surprising thing here is that the three gems are even more powerful than your immordilean!

I said- oh, I see, this might be the reason why the knight used the two metal rods instead of his hands! Fine I will try to destroy one of them you go fight devilen with whiturn, okay?

Angelias nodded and left. I pointed the immordilean towards one of the gems after looking at Angelias and whiturn for once.

I imagined that some power beams are coming out of the immordilean and it will destroy one of the gems at once.

The power beams had came out of the immordilean, but most of the things I imagined didn't actually happen!

I opened my eyes and saw that the power beam had touched the diamond gem! Remember what I had imagined- I had imagined that the power beams would come out of the immordilean and quickly it would destroy one of the gems, but it didn't quickly destroy it.

The beams definitely touched the gem but it didn't get destroyed quickly!

This might be happening because as Angelias said before- the diamond gem is the strongest gem than anything plus, in earth, the strongest element is the diamond itself!

I kept imagining the same thing which is- come on power beam you can do it, come on quickly!

But nothing had happened for a long while and in between something very-very bad happened!

Devilen saw what I was doing! He once again shouted- nooo, and then came running to me but somehow Angelias and whiturn managed to get him back!

Devilen tried his whole might to get away from Angelias and whiturn, as they were pulling him back and he was moving to the front. I could see that every second when he is being held behind, he was getting angrier and angrier!

Because of Devilens strength, he was coming nearer to me slowly-slowly every second!

The diamond gem which was being attacked by my power beam was glowing brightly every second!

Why did I choose the diamond gem? I should have chosen the ruby or the sapphire gem but I didn't have time think of that.

I kept focusing of the diamond gem, even though I couldn't see it because of its light!

Devilen now was only six steps away from me!

In between i could feeling like dad was saying-`oh-no' in my mind again and again.

Then soon a small crack was made in the diamond gem, yes I could see it blurrily.

I imagined that the immordilean was using its whole might to destroy it, and yes it happened, the yellow light coming from the immordilean glowed even brightly! Devilen even saw the crack of the diamond gem and the growing harmful power beam of the immordilean.

With that he got very angry and turned to whiturn and blasted powerful power beam out of his mouth which made whiturn and Angelias blast away from devilen! Then he quickly turned to me and came running to stop me!

Chapter-31

BOOOM!

When devilen was just two steps away from me, the entire diamond gem had lots of cracks on it and in a second.........BOOOM!

The diamond gem exploded with a big boom sound! Everyone got blasted away, but i only got eight steps away from the explosion as I protected myself by using my shield, while others including devilen had gone ninety steps away from me! Devilen shouted nooo extremely loud this time!

After the explosion something mysterious but nice thing happened!

Something came out from the dungeon of Devils Mountain, it was dust!

It looked same colour of the statue of devilen when he was a statue!

Devilen was now frightened and tried to run away. He was shouting `no' this whole time. The dust from the dungeon of Devil Mountain flew very fast towards devilen.

He flew with his wing trying to run away from the dust but it was no us, the dust soon touched devilen and it pulled him towards the mountain, and finally devilen entered the mountain!

We all who is me Angelias and whiturn expected devilen to come out of the mountain again but no.

Nothing happened for a while. We all decided to go inside that mountain and make sure that devilen won't come out.

Chapter-32

As it was before!

—•—

We all entered in the dungeon of Devil Mountain and kept walking but suddenly as we were walking the path ahead was dark!

I sighed and said now what? But suddenly the immordilean glowed brighly which made lights all around and it showed our way.

Whiturn suddenly said smiling- that's a great guardian of yours!

I smiled at him back. So, as we were walking we finally saw what we expected!

Yes, you thought that right! It was devilen, in the form of a statue as he was before!

And like before, it seemed like devilen was staring at me with an even angrier face! Whiturn squinted at him in an angry face.

Whiturn spoke to us- come on let's get out of here it is now as it was before!

We all came out of the mountain as soon as possible, and as we came out the immordilean glowed which made the door of the mountain close!

Suddenly someone had came to see us!

Chapter-33

The King and queen!

A door suddenly formed right in front of us! The door looked like it was made by some white diamond!

The door soon opened and what we was the king and queen! They both were having a very happy face.

They told all of us to come inside the castle after taking the left two gems which were lying in the ground. And we all did.

Now we all including whiturn was in the castle. The king came walking to me and gave me a hand shake and said- thank you so much for saving our world we both saw everything which you were doing and we very much appreciate your hard work of saving our world, and I even see that you brought back whiturn; now we would love to fulfill one of your beautiful dreams!

I smiled at the king and queen, then I said-actually I am happy that I came to this beautiful world and made friends in the heaven world and especially save the heaven world, I am proud that I did all these stuff so now I only want to go home which means I wish to go back to earth, and don't worry I promise that I will soon return.

The king smiled at me and said okay. Then he touched my immordilean which made the immordilean glow and soon a door appeared in front of me.

There, this door will lead you back to earth-said the king.

I said good bye to everyone to Angelias, to the king and queen, to whiturn and soon I passed through the door.

Chapter-34

Back home!

The door closed in front of me when I passed through it, and suddenly I fell out really quick!

Like the previous time everything around me was white, but this time I was falling down not flying. I didn't scream this time while falling because I knew I was going home!

While I was falling I passed through a door which suddenly appeared in front of me!

When I had just passed through the door everything around looked black. I somehow got relaxed.

It seemed like my eyes were closed and when I opened my eyes I saw that I was lying on the ground under a tree. It was night already!

I stood up slowly and started walking towards the place where everyone was, after sighing and saying- ah, this day was big and adventurous!

I reached the place where everyone was and waited there for a while.

Then suddenly it started to rain I ran to shades of a tree nearest to me. When I just leaned to the bark of the tree Jane came running to me!

I was so happy to see her. She came close to me and said- oh-no looks like I enjoyed too much, come on Gerald lets go home.

I smiled at her and we both started walking to our bikes. But there were many ways to go and it was too dark and rainy to find our bikes.

So, I looked upward at the rainy sky and suddenly one drop of water entered in both of my eyes!

I tried to remove it from my eyes but soon my eyes absorbed it. And suddenly something strange happened!

One of the ways started to glow! It was like I just used the mapper drop!

I turned to Jane and said- hey, do you see that? She replied- see what?

After she said that, I realized that I was having the mapper drop! I looked at the sky again covering my eyes, and maybe it was imagination but I saw Angelias winking his eyes at me!

I smiled at him back followed the glowing way after telling Jane to follow me. And soon we reached home, I went to bed and slept after a while, and I dreamed that Angelias, whiturn and I were once again in the heaven world enjoying out there!

Chapter-35

Meanwhile in the devil kingdom

King Daredevil said to himself-no-no this cannot be happening, I will take revenge from them soon, wait let me think.

Suddenly the knight whom we had fought came nearer to him with a sad face- your majesty what will do now? We cannot even bring devilen back to life!

With that daredevil stopped thinking and said- that's it! Yes I got a plan and this time they cannot do anything to stop me.

The knight asked- so, what is the new plan? The king cackled! You will know that just wait and watch! HA-HA-HA-HA-HAA!

THE END

ABOUT THE AUTHOR

The author's name is SUHAAN.J.KRISHNAN. He was born in Maharashtra, Pune. In 2007, June 21. His mother's name is JIJITHA.KRISHNAN, she is a single parent. Suhaan started trying to be an author ever since he was 12 years old. He first thought to write a short story first, but then he changed his mind and decided to write a long story like this one. After his studies, he gets short breaks, at that time he sometimes thinks about the story he is writing and what stories he should make. Even at night when he is not sleepy, he thinks of a good story and writes his ideas in his laptop. He was only 13 years old when he wrote this story. One of his dreams is to become a great author, and help the people who is poor and does not have enough money to live there life's. He will help the poor people by giving them some of the money he received by publishing his books. He really is thankful to you all for choosing this book and he promise to you that the next book will also be as amazing like this one. Thank you!

THANK YOU!

www.ingramcontent.com/pod-product-compliance
Lightning Source LLC
Chambersburg PA
CBHW051225160726
47994CB00002B/754